ADAPTED BY
Teresa Mlawer

ILLUSTRATED BY
Olga Cuéllar

Goldilocks and the Three Bears

Adirondack
Books

Once upon a time there was a girl with beautiful curly golden hair, who everyone called Goldilocks. She lived in a small house with a garden near a green forest. She loved to help her parents, so one day she set out to find wood to build a fire.

She walked a long way and soon became lost in the forest. After much wandering she came across a log cabin with smoke coming out of its chimney. She figured there must be someone in the house who could help her find her way back home, so she knocked on the door, but no one answered.

She waited a while, and after realizing the door was unlocked, decided to go inside.

"Is there anyone home?" she asked from the hall.

When no one answered, she went into the kitchen.
On top of a big wooden table she found three bowls:
a big bowl, a medium bowl, and a very small bowl,
all filled with rich porridge topped with honey.

By now, Goldilocks was very hungry, so she tasted the
porridge from the big bowl, but it was much too hot.

Then, she tasted the porridge from the medium bowl, but it was much too cold. Finally, she tasted the porridge from the small bowl, and it was just right. It was so delicious that she ate the entire bowl of porridge.

Afterwards, Goldilocks went into the living room and saw a bookcase full of books and three chairs: a big chair, a medium chair, and a very small chair. She decided to sit and read a book while waiting for the owners of the house to return.

First, Goldilocks tried to sit on the big chair, but it was so high that she could not reach it. Then, she sat in the medium chair, but it was too wide and not very comfortable. Finally, she sat in the small chair and it was just right, but she flopped herself down so hard that it broke!

After reading for a while, Goldilocks became sleepy, so she decided to go the bedroom. There she found three beds in a row: a big bed, a medium bed, and a very small bed. She went to lie down on the big bed but it was much too hard.

Then, she lay down on the medium bed, but it was much
too soft. Finally, she lay down on the small bed and it was
just right. Soon she fell into a deep sleep.

While Goldilocks was asleep, the family of bears that lived in the house returned home.

They had gone out for a walk while their porridge with honey cooled down. The Papa Bear was very big, the Mama Bear was medium sized, and their son, Baby Bear, was very small. They saw that the door was open and realized that someone had gone into their house.

When they entered the kitchen, they approached the table.

"SOMEONE HAS TASTED MY PORRIDGE!" said Papa Bear.

"SOMEONE HAS TASTED MY PORRIDGE TOO!" said Mama Bear.

"SOMEONE HAS EATEN MY PORRIDGE!" cried Baby Bear.

The three bears were very surprised because they always went for a walk before breakfast and nothing like this had ever happened before.

They lived in a quiet place in the forest, and the closest neighbors always called before coming by. Cautiously, they decided to check the rest of the house, so they went to the living room.

When they entered the living room, they saw that someone
had moved their chairs.

"SOMEONE HAS MOVED MY CHAIR!" said Papa Bear.

"SOMEONE HAS BEEN SITTING ON MY CHAIR!" said Mama Bear.

"SOMEONE HAS BROKEN MY CHAIR!" cried Baby Bear.

Next, they went to the bedroom. When they approached the big bed, Papa Bear said:

"SOMEONE HAS BEEN LYING IN MY BED!"

When they approached the middle bed, Mama Bear said:

"SOMEONE HAS BEEN LYING IN MY BED TOO!"

When they approached the small bed they saw a girl
with golden locks sound asleep.

Baby Bear screamed with all his might:

"SOMEONE IS SLEEPING IN MY BED!!"

Upon hearing the screams, Goldilocks woke up. When she saw the three bears staring down at her, she got so frightened that she jumped out of the bed, and flew out the window. She started running and she didn't stop until she found her way back home.

Meanwhile, the bears just looked at each other in confusion. They couldn't understand why the girl with the golden locks had been so frightened. They tried to stop her to find out who she was, but Goldilocks was running so fast that it was impossible to catch up to her.

When Goldilocks got home, she told her parents what happened and promised them she would never wander that far from home again. That night, after reading a bedtime story with her parents, she said to them:

"I'm very sorry I ate Baby Bear's porridge. Maybe we can invite the bears over to our house one day for some of Mama's delicious blueberry pie."

FOR INFORMATION, PLEASE CONTACT ADIRONDACK BOOKS, P.O. BOX 266, CANANDAIGUA, NEW YORK 14424

ISBN 978-0-9898934-0-4   CJ 10 9 8 7 6 5 4 3   PRINTED IN CHINA